RICHARD SCARRY'S
Great Big Schoolhouse
Readers

Kooky Campout

Illustrated by Huck Scarry
Written by Erica Farber

STERLING CHILDREN'S BOOKS
New York

It was the first day
of summer. Hooray!
Lowly wanted to
play marbles.

Skip wanted to
play ball.

Arthur wanted to play cards.

"Let's go camping!" said Huckle.

Huckle got a tent.

Skip got sleeping bags.

Lowly got fishing poles.

Arthur got snacks.

The boys set up the tent in
the backyard.

In went the sleeping bags.

In went the snacks. In went the boys.

Don't eat all the chips, Arthur!

CRASH! The tent fell.

The girls looked over the fence.

"What are you doing?"

asked Bridget.

"Camping," said Huckle. "We are

going to sleep in our tent."

"We want to go

camping, too,"

said Ella.

"We want to sleep in our tent,
too," said Molly and Frances.

The girls set up their tent next door.

They put lots of things inside.

Ella and Molly had a tea party.

Arthur came, too.

"Would you like a cookie?" Ella
asked her doll.

"Yes," said Arthur. "I love cookies."

Then they had a pillow fight.

OOPS! Look out for the teacups!

The boys went fishing.

"I'm going to catch that fish," said Skip.

"I'm going to catch it," said Huckle.

"That is not a fish," said Molly.

"That is a shoe."

"I got it!" said Arthur.

"I got it!" said Lowly.

SPLASH! The boys fell into the pool! The shoe flew up in the air.

"We got it!" yelled the girls.

After dinner, it was time to catch fireflies.

Oh, no! Look where you are going, Huckle!

Mrs. Cat made them a campfire.

They roasted marshmallows.

Something strange ran by.

"It's a monster!" yelled Ella.

She bumped into Arthur. Oh, no!

Marshmallows went everywhere!

"That is not a monster," said
Bridget. "That is Arthur's lizard."
Then Lowly told a ghost joke.
Everyone laughed.

Molly told a ghost story.

"Once there was a ghost called
Kooky. Kooky was very spooky.
Kooky the Spooky Ghost came
out at night. Do you know
what Kooky said?"

"What?" asked Frances.

"I want a kooky! *Kooky* is how
Kooky the Spooky Ghost
said cookie."

CRASH! Everyone looked up.
They saw a spooky shadow.
CRUNCH! CRUNCH!
The spooky shadow was
eating something.
"It's Kooky the Spooky Ghost!"
said Molly.

AAAHHH! Everyone ran outside.
They saw cookies on the ground.
"It's Kooky the Spooky Ghost!"
they all yelled.

"Look!" said Huckle.

He pointed to the tent.

A small shape was standing in front
of it. The small shape was eating
a cookie. When it moved, the big
shadow on the tent moved.

"It's Arthur's lizard!" said Bridget.

20

"You know what I am going to call him?" said Arthur. "Kooky Spooky!"

Huckle and his friends camped in Huckle's house. They slept in their tent all night long. So did Kooky Spooky.

Kooky Spooky was not kooky or spooky, but it sure was a kooky spooky campout!

STERLING CHILDREN'S BOOKS
New York

An Imprint of Sterling Publishing
387 Park Avenue South
New York, NY 10016

ISBN 978-1-4027-9914-3 (hardcover)
ISBN 978-1-4027-9915-0 (paperback)

Produced by

 JR Sansevere

Distributed in Canada by Sterling Publishing
℅ Canadian Manda Group, 664 Annette Street,
Toronto, Ontario, Canada M6S 2C8w
Distributed in the United Kingdom by GMC Distribution Services
Castle Place, 166 High Street, Lewes, East Sussex, England BN7 1XU
Distributed in Australia by Capricorn Link (Australia) Pty. Ltd.
P.O. Box 704, Windsor, NSW 2756, Australia

For information about custom editions, special sales, premium and corporate purchases,
please contact Sterling Special Sales at 800-805-5489 or specialsales@sterlingpublishing.com.

Manufactured in China

Lot #:
2 4 6 8 10 9 7 5 3 1
11/14

www.sterlingpublishing.com/kids